Hello!

Congratulations, on taking your first step into the music world.

The Divertimento Music course is designed to support beginner musicians who are ready to learn the fundamental basics of piano and music.

In Book one, you will be learning easy music theory and piano that will train your ability to read basic notes and concepts of music.

I hope you enjoy your music journey with the Divertimento Music Course as much as I did writing the book!

-Mikaela Dodge

Finding Middle C

Knowing where middle "C" is on the piano and sheet music is a crucial part of piano and music learning.

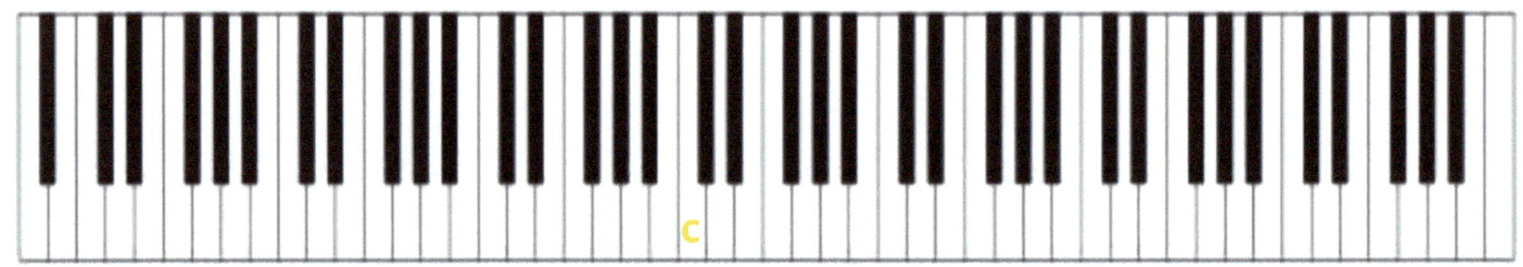

Learning Finger numbers

Before getting started with playing the piano, it is important you learn your finger numbers for the right and left hand.

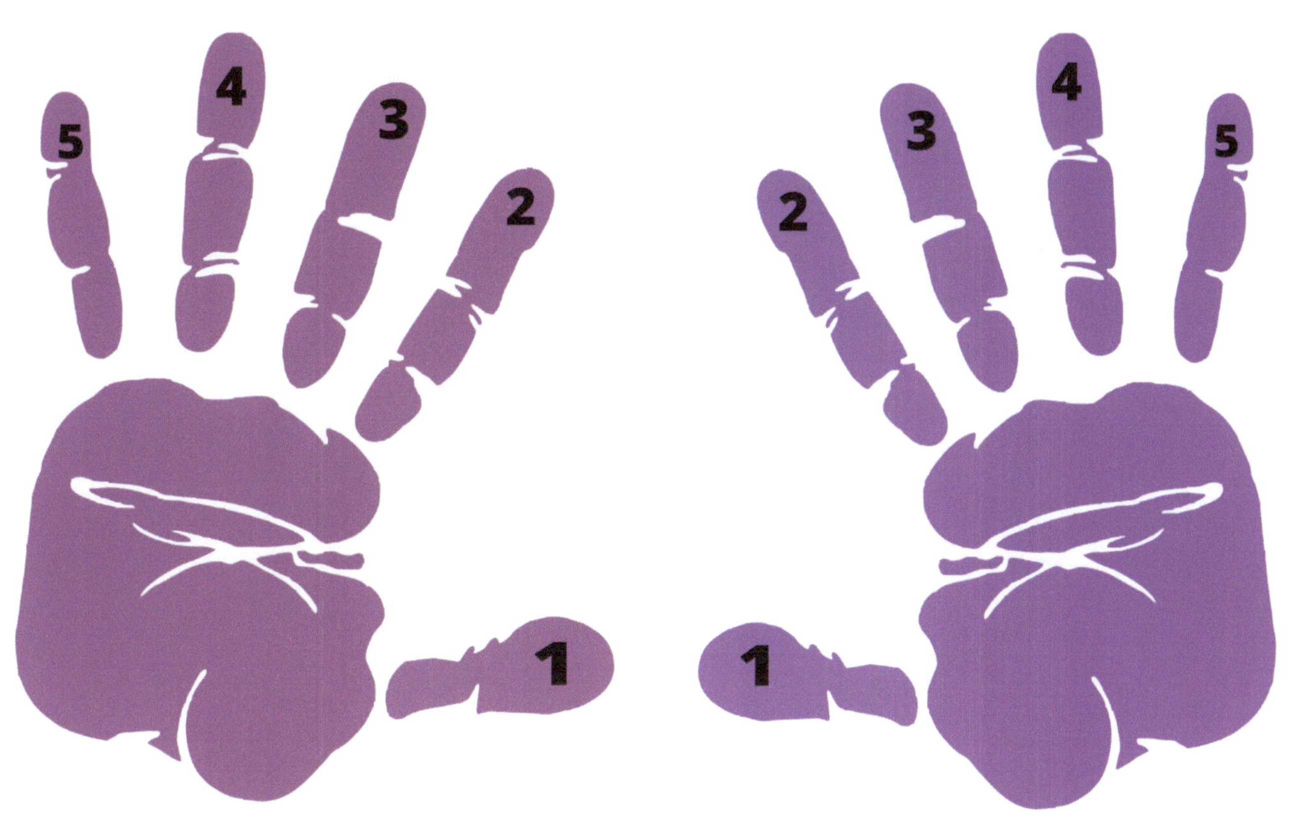

Learning Piano Keys

✴ Activity: -Circle all the black keys that are grouped in twos.

-Box all black keys that are grouped in threes.

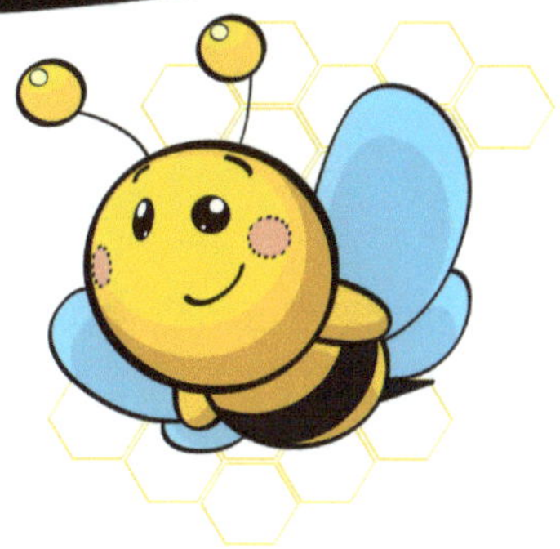

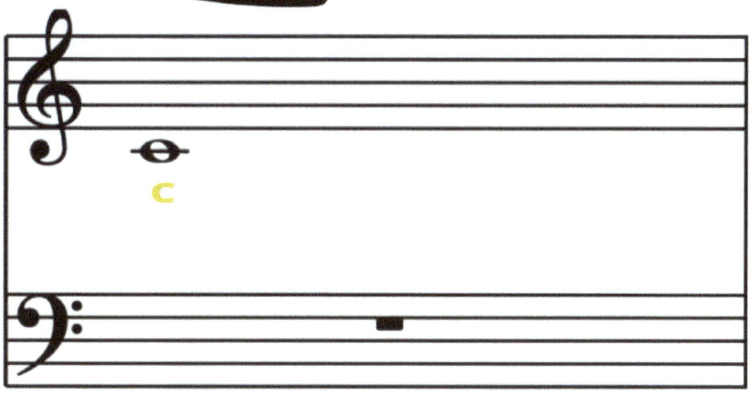

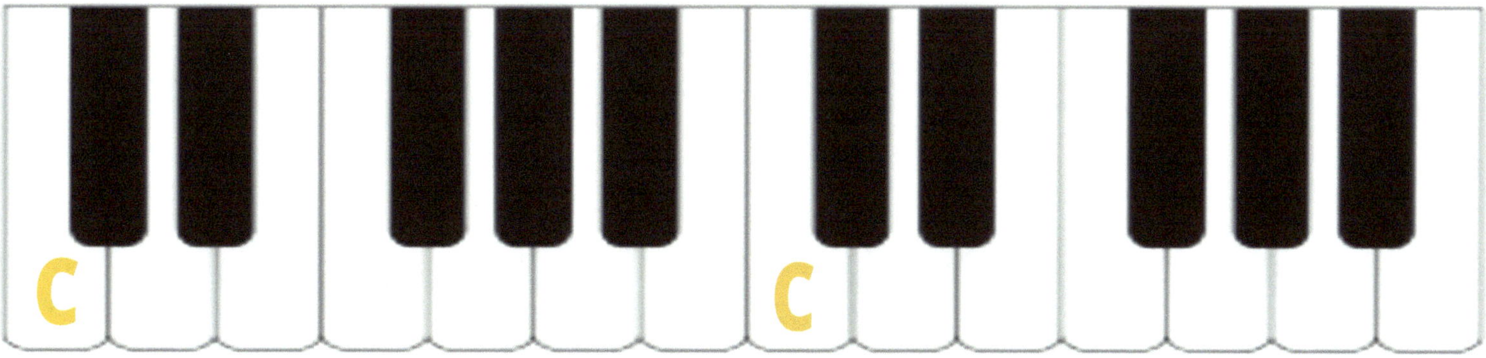

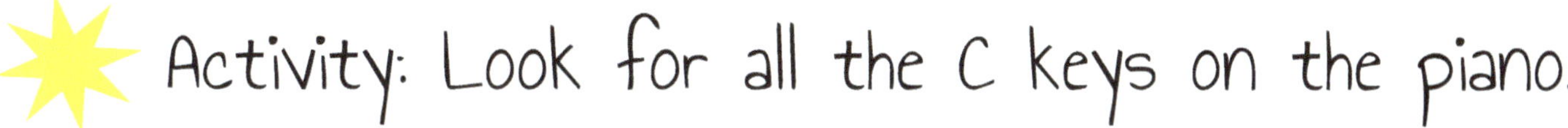

Activity: Look for all the C keys on the piano.

The next 2 notes after "C"
on the piano are "D" and "E."

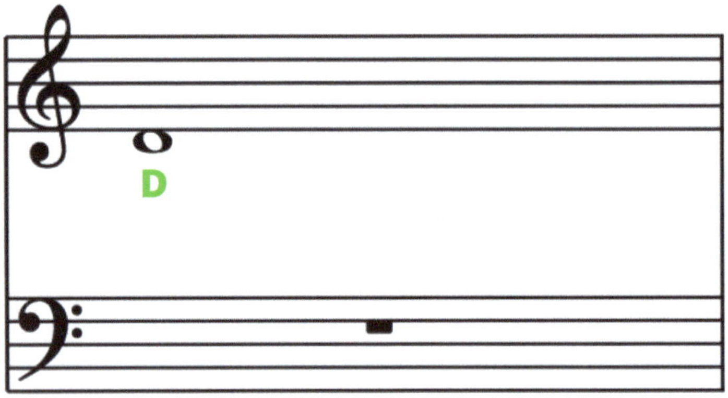

D

E

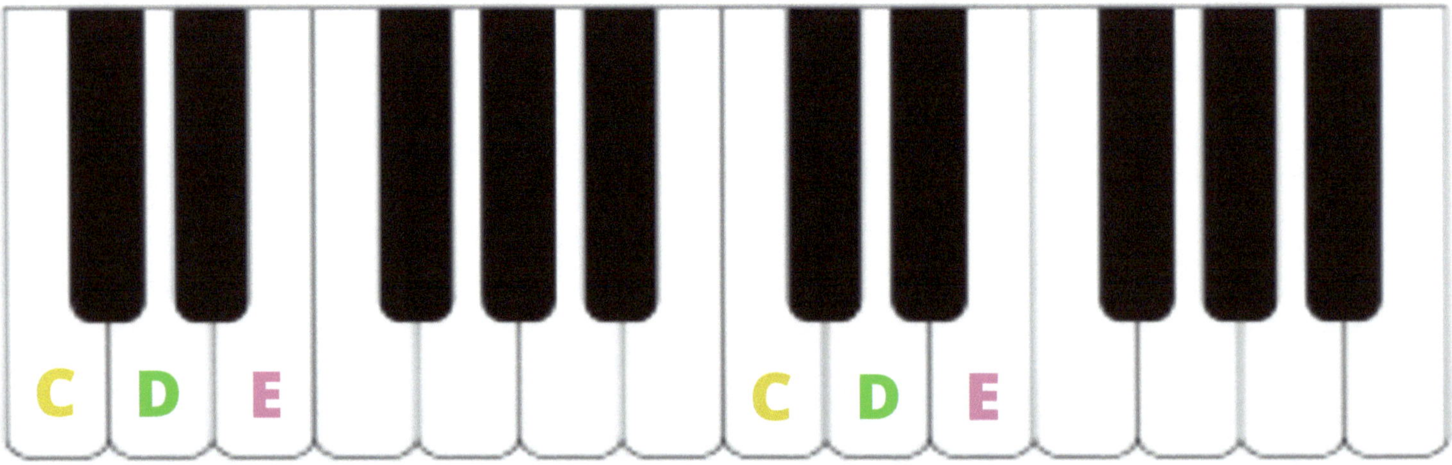

C D E
C D E

The next 2 notes after "E" are "F" and "G."
F
G
C D E F G C D E F G

Lastly, the 2 letters after "G" are "A" and "B."
A
B
C D E F G A B C D E F G A B

Reading music notes

When musicians read notes for music, they read musical notes on staff lines.

The staffs are divided by two parts which are called:

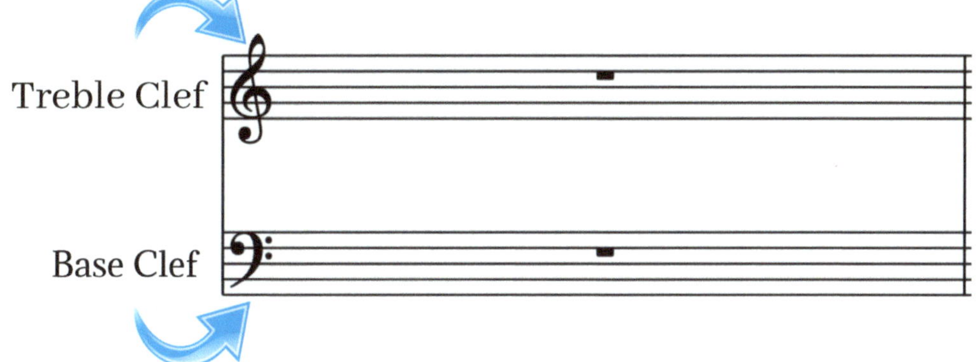

Time signatures are given in the beginning of a composition/song to show how many beats are going to be in a measure.

In this book we will only be using 4/4

Below is the C scale on a staff in the Treble and Base clef.

It is important to know what letter the notes are on the staff. Being able to understand the notes will kick start your piano playing and music journey.

Piano Playing
using finger #'s 1 and 2

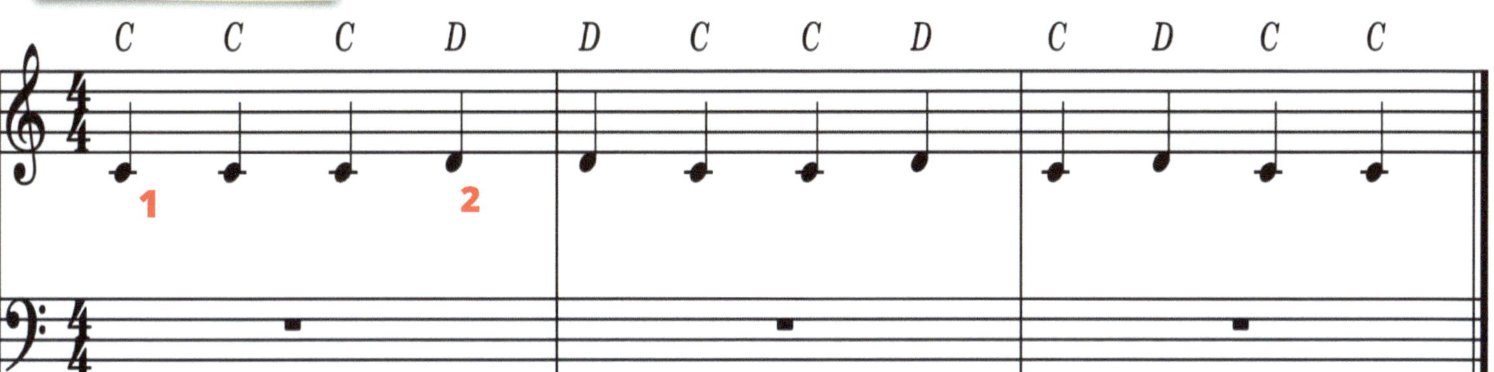

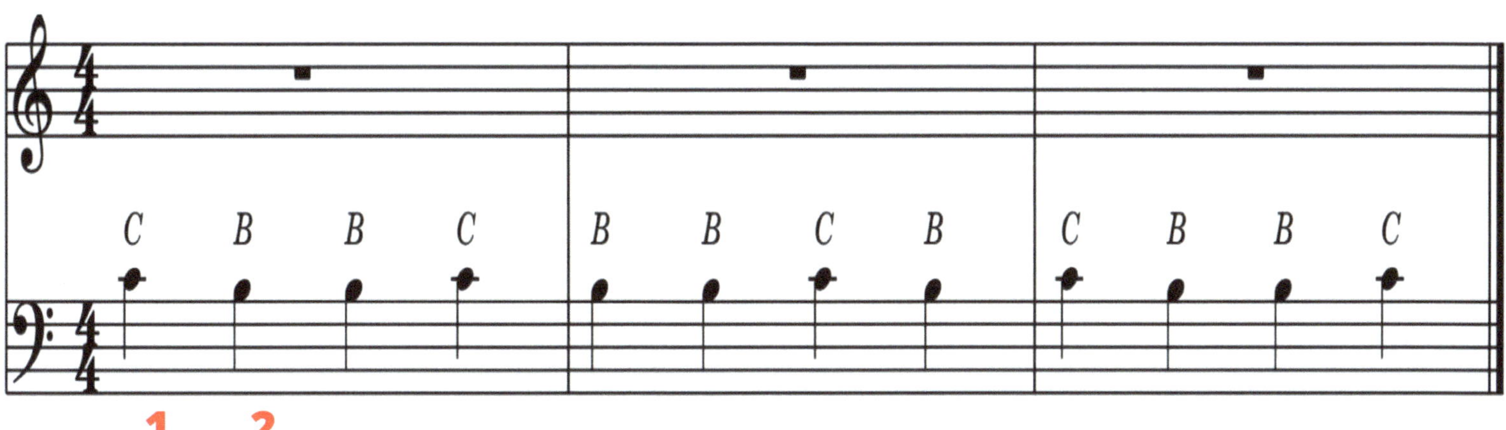

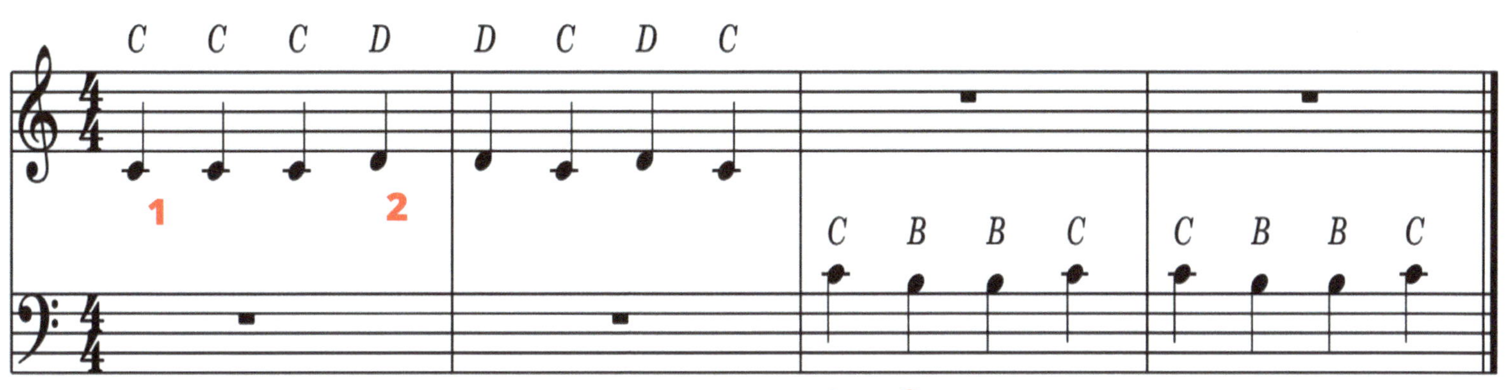

Piano Playing

adding finger #'s 3 and 4

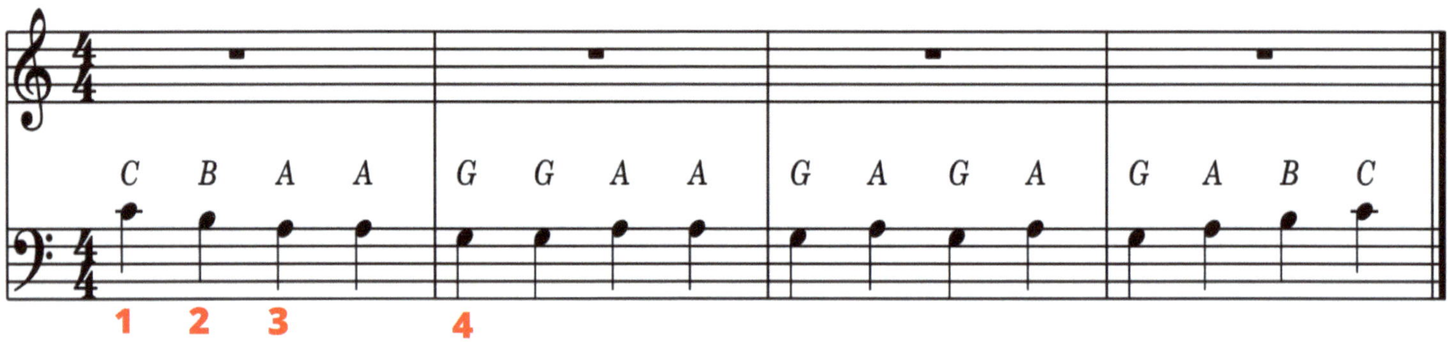

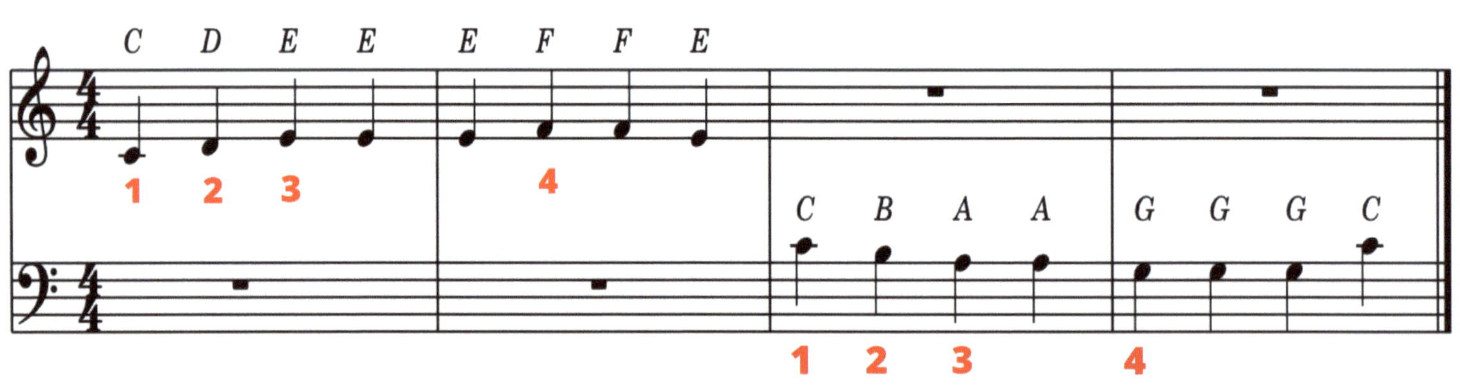

Piano Playing
using finger # 5

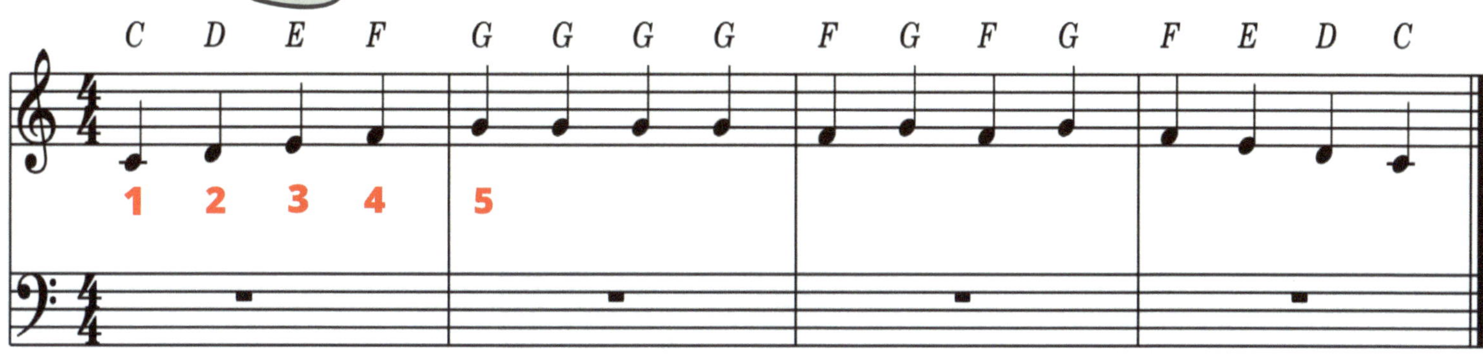

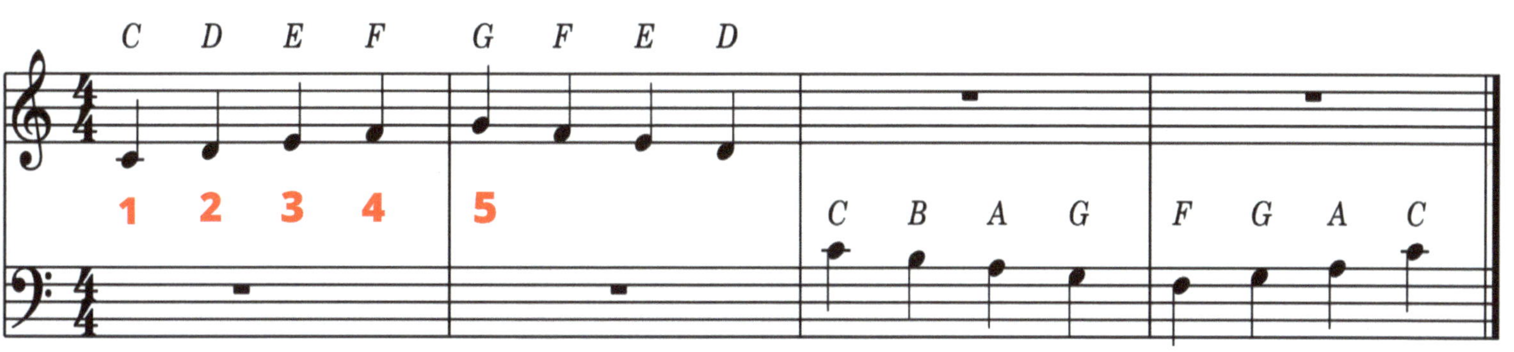

Activity for note letters C-G
on the Treble clef

Write the letter of the notes under each measure.

Activity for note letter C-G

on the Bass clef 𝄢

Write the letter under each musical note.

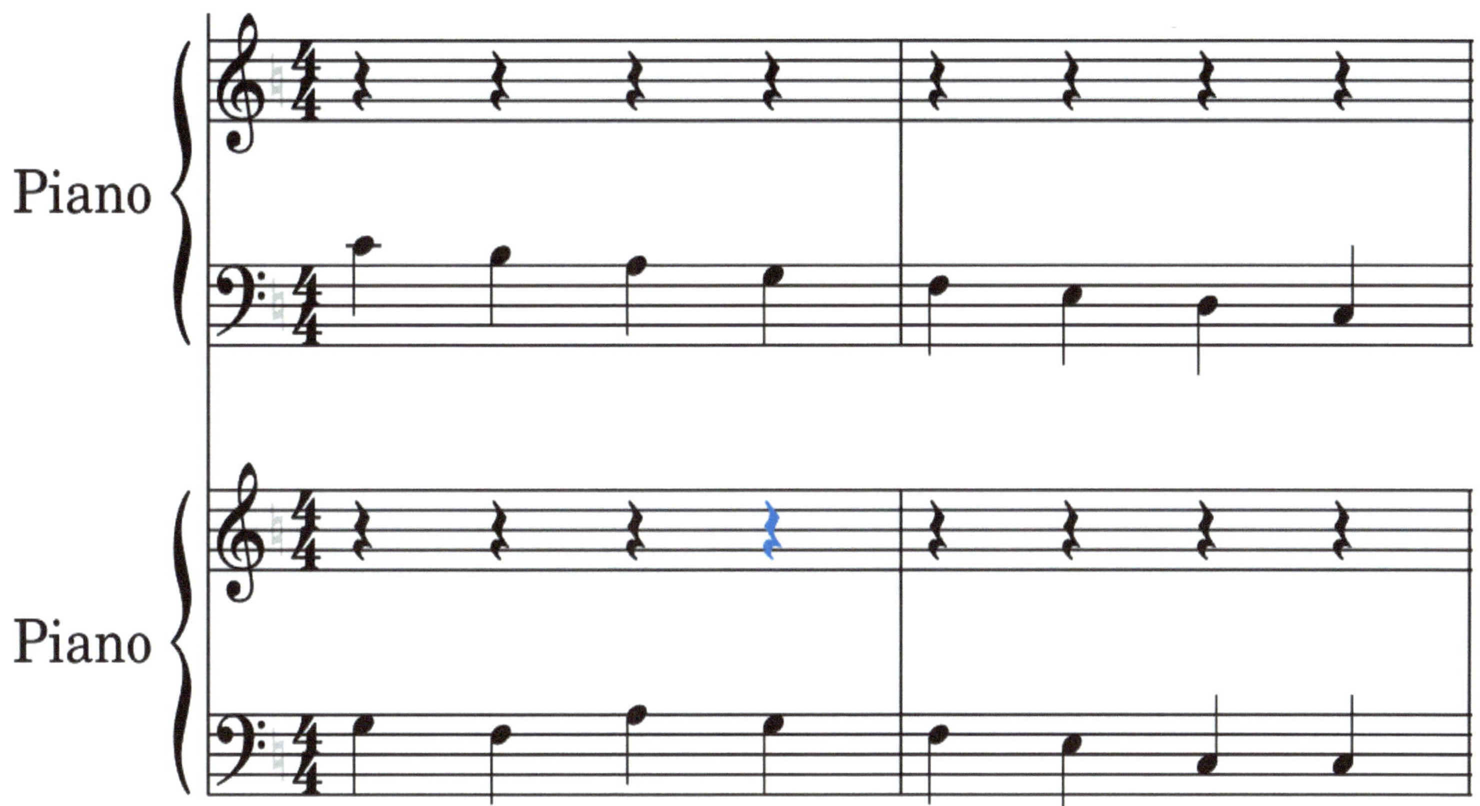

Now you are ready to start playing the first song!

Piano

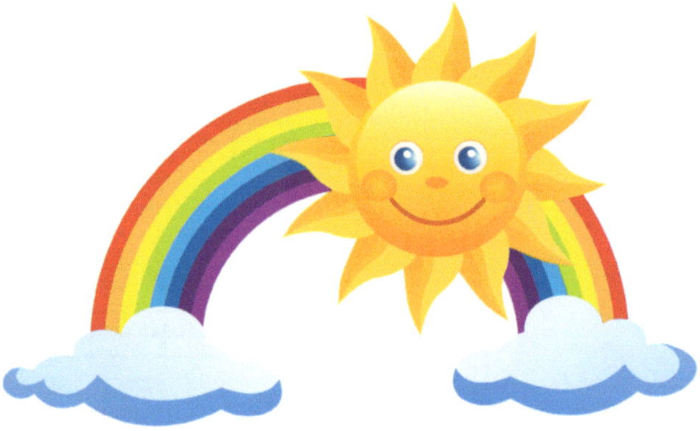

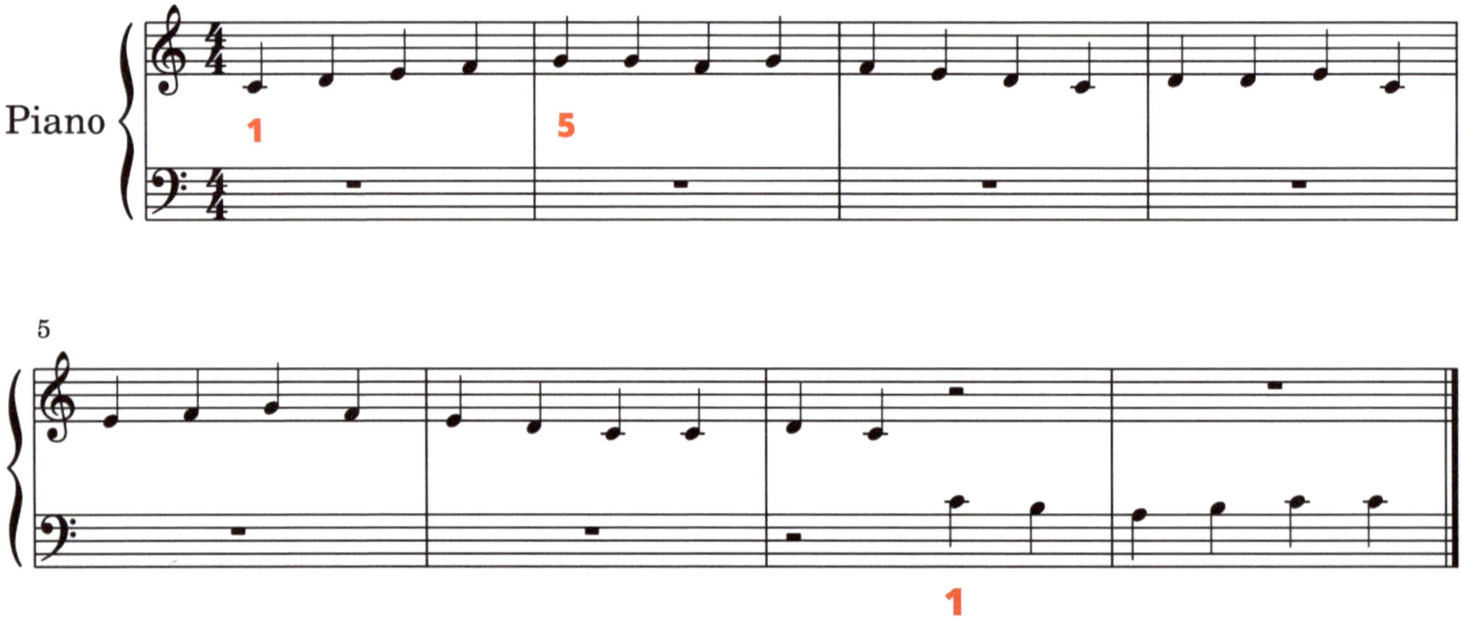

Mountain Top

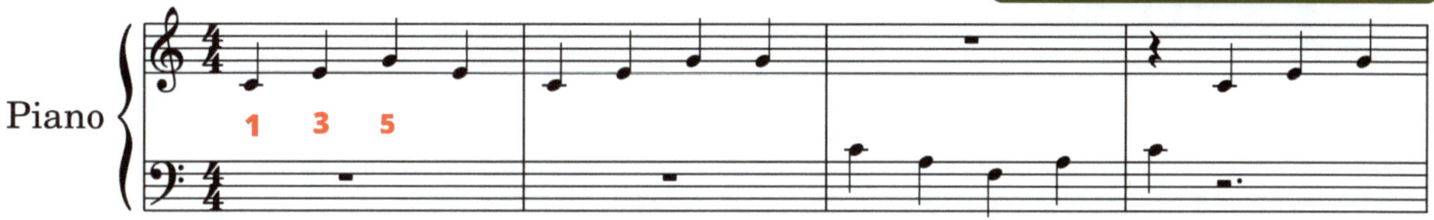

Ballerina Shoes

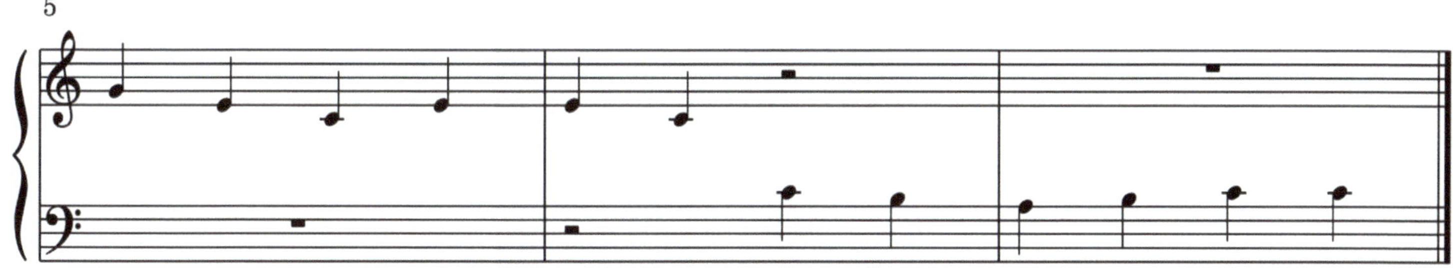

Musical Notes

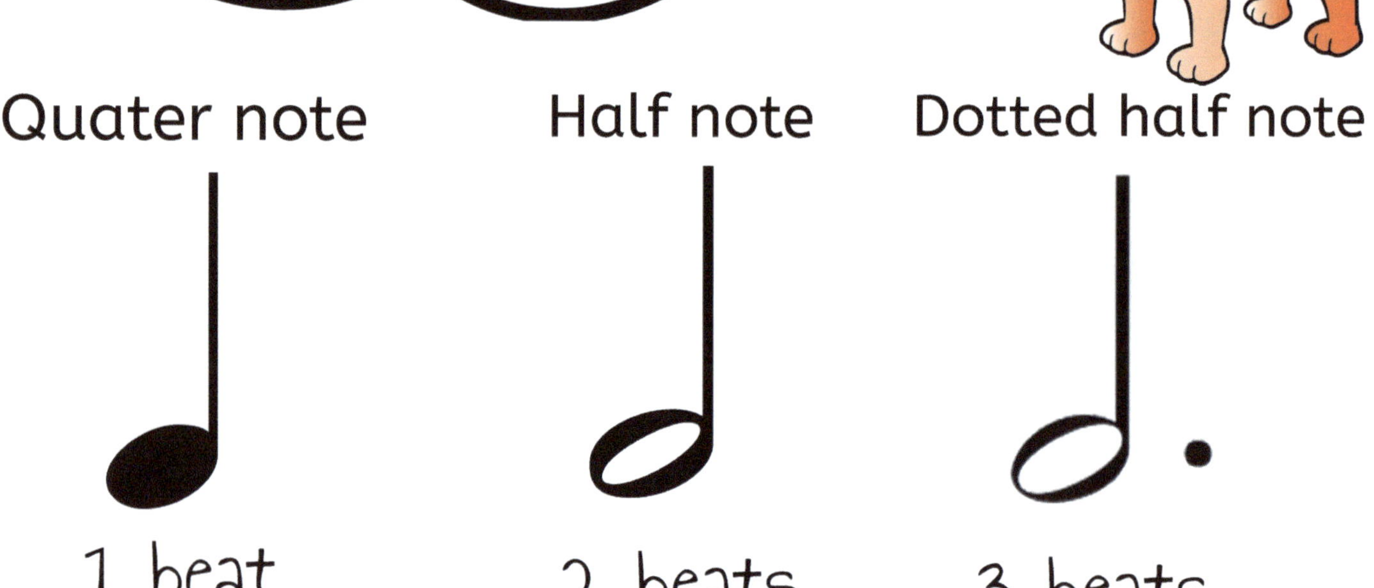

whole note

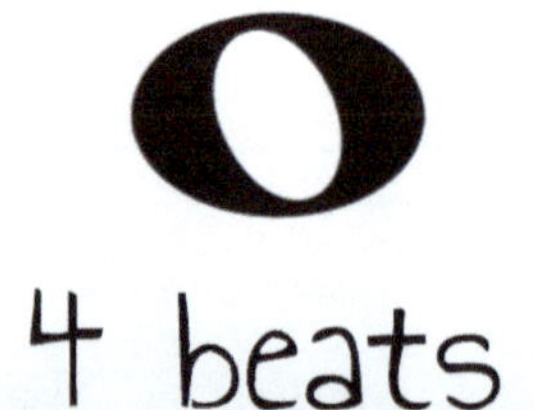

Under each note, write the beats that are connected with the note.

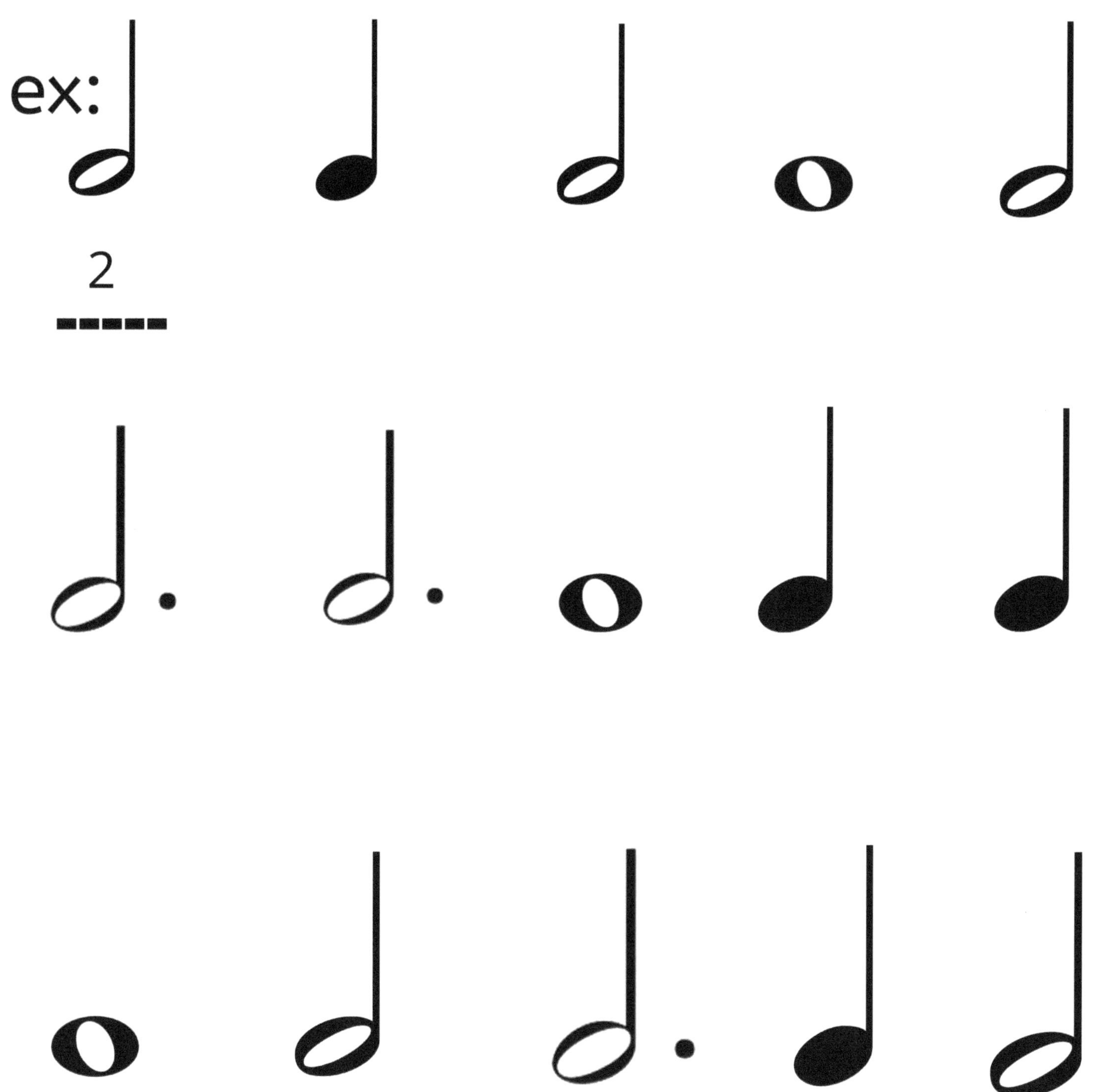

Playing with counts

Now it is time to practice piano with the proper beats!

Kitty Cat

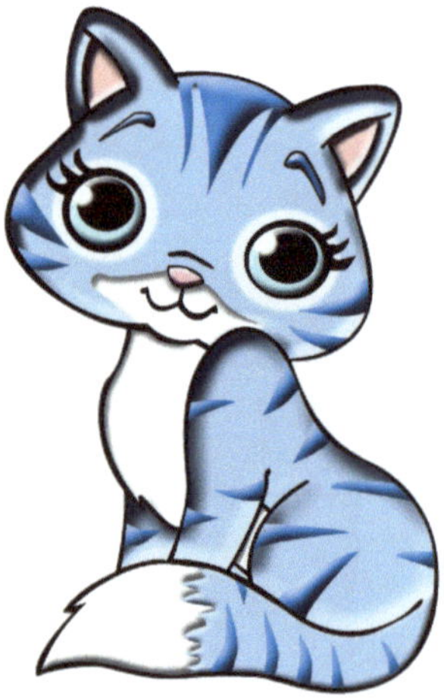

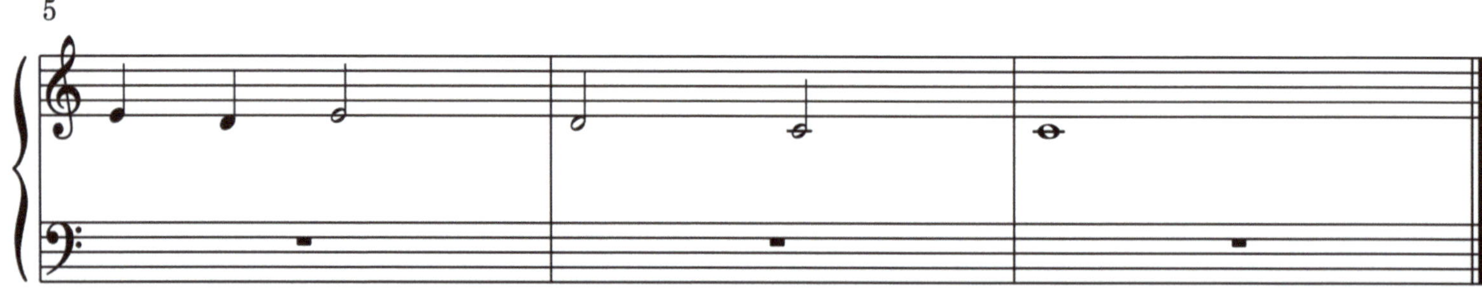

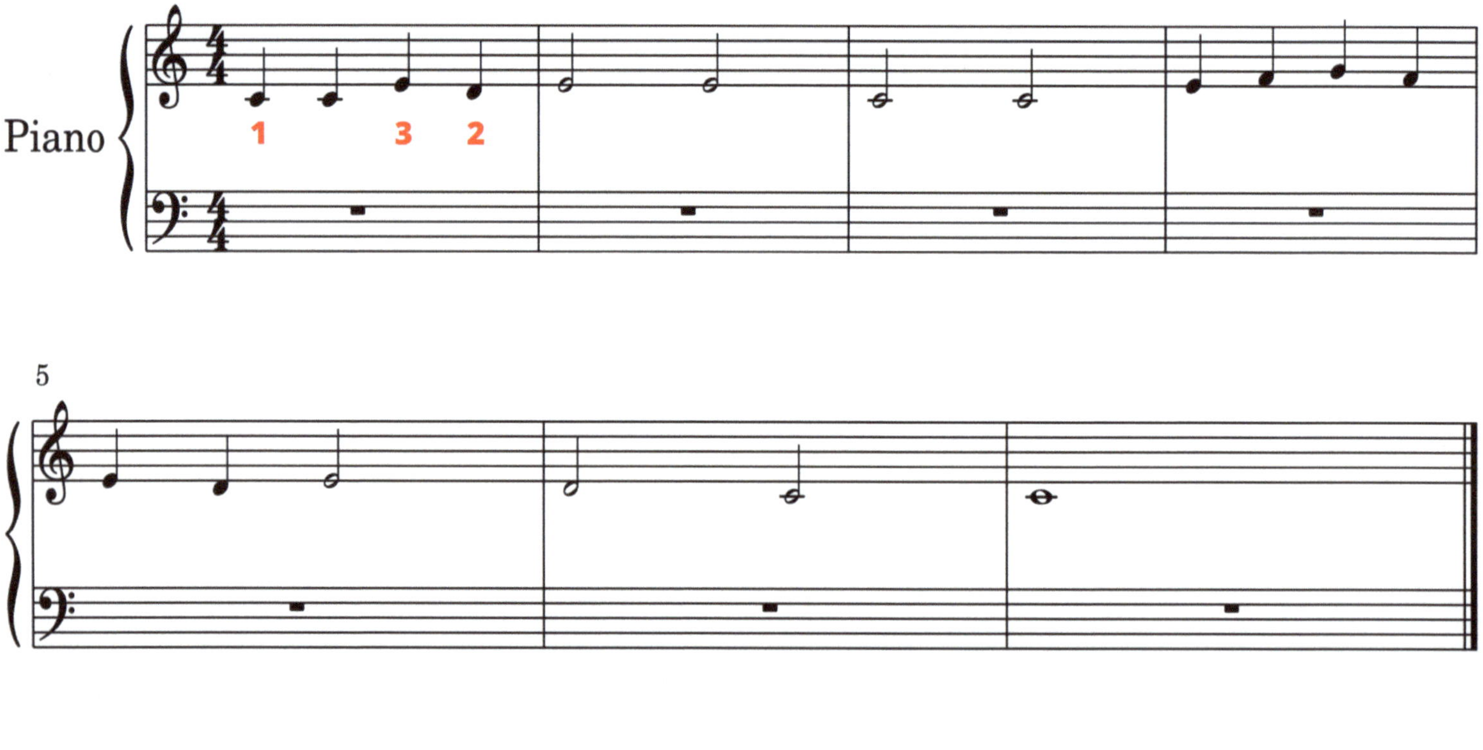

Silly Cow

Little River

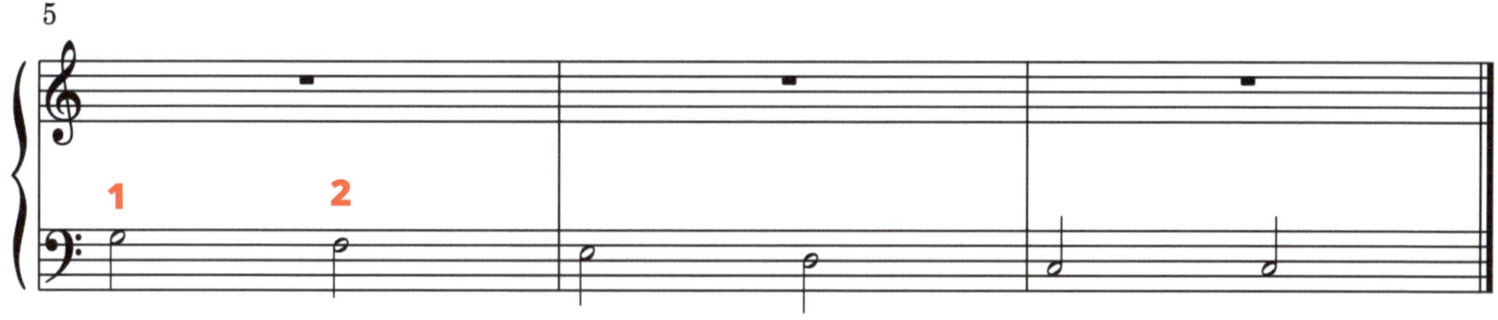

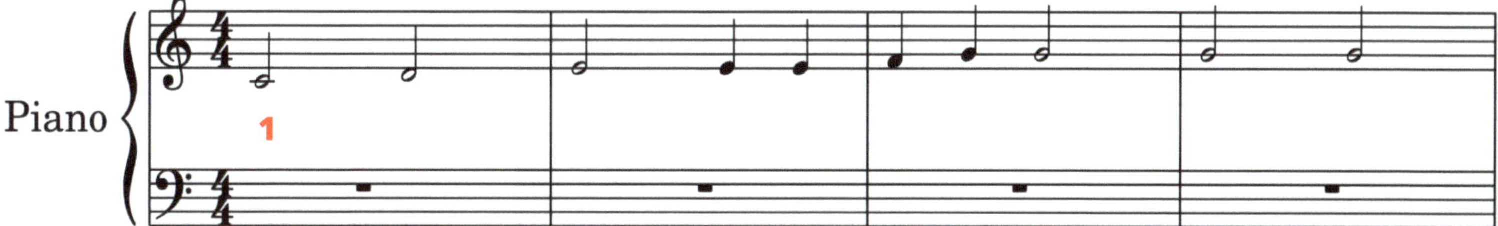

Pencil Tip
Piano
5
Cassette
Piano
5

Activity for whole notes

Draw 4 whole notes 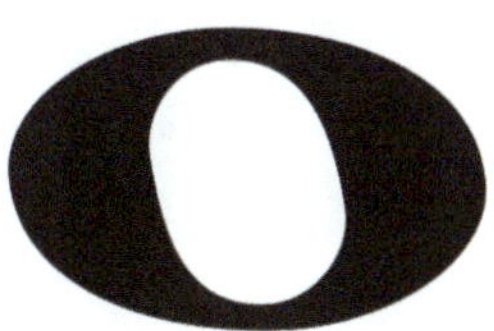

Activity for half notes

Draw 4 half notes

Activity for dotted half notes

Draw 4 dotted half notes 𝅗𝅥.

Activity for quater notes

Draw 4 quater notes ♩

Musical Notes Activity

Circle all quater notes.

Heart all whole notes.

Square all half notes.

Line all dotted half notes.

Silver Rain

Piano

Contrary Motion Excersize

Piano

Last Song